Twelfth Night

by William Shakespeare

Retold by Steve Barlow and Steve Skidmore

Illustrated by Catherine Ward

Series Editors: Steve Barlow and Steve Skidmore

Heinemann

Published by Heinemann Educational Publishers
Halley Court, Jordan Hill, Oxford OX2 8EJ
A division of Reed Educational and Professional Publishing Ltd

OXFORD   MELBOURNE   AUCKLAND
JOHANNESBURG   BLANTYRE   GABORONE
IBADAN   PORTSMOUTH NH (USA)   CHICAGO

First published 2000
2004   2003   2002   2001   2000
10 9 8 7 6 5 4 3 2 1
ISBN 0 435 21394 6

Illustrations by Catherine Ward
Cover design by Shireen Nathoo Design
Cover artwork by John Holder
Designed by Artistix, Thame, Oxon
Printed and bound in Great Britain by Athenaeum Press Ltd

Tel: 01865 888058 www.heinemann.co.uk

Contents

Characters   4

A beginning   6

Chapter 1   Shipwrecked!   8

Chapter 2   Knights behaving badly   11

Chapter 3   The Duke in love   14

Chapter 4   Olivia   17

Chapter 5   Back from the dead   23

Chapter 6   The kill-joy   28

Chapter 7   A love letter   31

Chapter 8   Sir Andrew's challenge   39

Chapter 9   Malvolio goes mad   43

Chapter 10   The duel   47

Chapter 11   Mistaken identity   53

Chapter 12   Twelfth night   55

An ending   63

Characters

Viola (pronounced Vie-oh-lah) – who disguises herself as a boy called Cesario (Sez-ar-ee-oh)

Sebastian – Viola's twin brother

Duke Orsino (Or-seen-oh) – in love with Olivia

Countess Olivia – in mourning for her dead brother

Sir Toby Belch – Olivia's drunken uncle

Sir Andrew Aguecheek (Aig-yew-cheek) – a foolish, rich knight (who is being used by Sir Toby)

Feste (Fess-tay) – Olivia's jester

Malvolio – Olivia's steward (a bore!)

Maria – Olivia's maid

Fabian (Fay-bee-an) – a friend of Sir Toby and a deadly enemy of Malvolio

Antonio – a friend of Sebastian and an enemy of Duke Orsino

A BEGINNING

The wind howled.

Thunder rolled.

Lightning split the sky.

The storm had torn the ship's sails to rags. Great waves broke across the deck. The helpless ship drifted towards needle-sharp rocks.

Another wall of water smashed into the ship. Viola watched in horror as her brother was swept away from her. She saw his fingers clutching at the ship's rail.

"Sebastian!" she cried.

Then he was gone.

Moments later, the doomed ship was hurled onto the rocks.

Viola was thrown into the sea. Salt water filled her eyes and her mouth. She thought

she felt strong hands grasp her shoulders. But
then darkness swept over her, and she knew
no more.

CHAPTER 1

Shipwrecked!

Viola opened her eyes.

The storm was over.

She looked around. The sky was dark, but the sea was calm.

She lay on a beach, beside a fire made of driftwood. The captain of her ship sat on the other side of the fire.

Slowly, Viola sat up. She turned to the captain.

Viola had never heard of Illyria. Her eyes filled with tears. Her brother Sebastian was drowned and she had no money. She was on her own.

"What can I do?" Viola asked.

"You could go to the Countess Olivia," replied the Captain. "But I don't think she'd help you. She hasn't seen anyone since her brother died a year ago. She won't even see the Duke."

"What is his name?"

"Duke Orsino. He's madly in love with the Countess. You could go to him for help."

"And beg from him?" Viola shook her head angrily. "Let him think that I'm a helpless female who can't look after myself?"

There was a pause as an idea grew in Viola's head. "I could be his servant."

The captain shook his head. "He's not married. He has no women servants."

Viola smiled. "He won't know I'm a woman." The captain looked puzzled.

"Will you help me, captain?" asked Viola. "Find me some men's clothes. I'll pretend I'm a page-boy! He'll never suspect a thing!"

The captain shook his head, but Viola soon talked him round.

She was that sort of person.

CHAPTER 2

Knights behaving badly

The Countess Olivia had an uncle called Sir Toby Belch.

Sir Toby had spent all his money on drink. When that was gone, he had spent Olivia's money on drink, until she wouldn't let him have any more.

"My niece is always unhappy these days," Sir Toby complained to Olivia's maid, Maria. "I think she must like being miserable."

Maria glared at him. "She's angry because you are always coming home drunk with your awful friend."

Sir Toby gave her a hard stare. "Do you mean Sir Andrew Aguecheek?"

"Yes, I do! He's a fool."

"Ssh!" ordered Sir Toby. "Here he comes! Off you go."

As Maria hurried away, Sir Andrew wandered in. Sir Toby staggered to his feet and bowed. Sir Andrew returned the greeting.

"Good Sir Andrew. You look sad."

"I am going home tomorrow, Sir Toby," Sir Andrew replied.

This was bad news for Sir Toby. Sir Andrew was very rich, and very foolish. Sir Andrew had given Sir Toby a lot of money. This was because Sir Toby had promised Sir Andrew that Olivia would fall in love with him.

Why are you going?

What chance have I got with Olivia when the Duke loves her?

Don't worry, she won't marry the Duke.

Sir Andrew's frown disappeared at once. "Oh, well, I'll stay another month then." He jumped up and began to dance about. "Sometimes I change my mind just like that!" he said happily.

Sir Toby pretended to be impressed. "What a dancer!" he cried. "Let's see you leap!"

Sir Andrew gave a feeble jump.

"Excellent!" roared Sir Toby. "Higher! Ha-ha! Higher!"

Sir Andrew hopped and grew red in the face. Sir Toby clapped and cheered him on. And Olivia watched them and wished the earth would open up and swallow them both.

CHAPTER 3

The Duke in love

Viola had been as good as her word. She had dressed as a page boy, and gone to Duke Orsino's palace. She had told the Duke that her name was Cesario. The Duke had been fooled by Viola's disguise and had given her a job. Her cheery nature had quickly made her the Duke's favourite servant.

Viola lay on her bed. She heard Orsino calling.

"Cesario! Cesario!"

Viola sat up with a jerk.

"Cesario! Where are you?" The Duke was calling for her! She struggled into her page-boy's jacket and rushed to the Great Hall.

The Duke was lying on a sofa, listening to his musicians play a sad song.

He looked up and saw Viola.

Viola felt angry with her master. He was young, rich and handsome. But he spent every minute of the day groaning and moaning about how much he loved Olivia. Viola wanted to shake him.

"Cesario, I want you to go to Olivia."
The Duke took hold of Viola's hand. Viola
felt her heart flutter a little.

"Say that you won't leave until she sees
you," Orsino continued.

"If I do see her, my lord, what shall I say?"

Orsino gripped Viola's hand tighter. "Tell
her how much I love her. She will listen to
you. You are young. You must know what it is
like to be in love."

"Yes, my lord," whispered Viola.

"Then go quickly."

Viola hurried away. But as soon as she
was out of sight, she stopped. She leaned
against a wall and groaned.

Cesario was Duke Orsino's servant. A
servant must do what he is told.

But how could Viola persuade Olivia to
love Duke Orsino, when she had fallen in
love with Orsino herself?

CHAPTER 4

Olivia

At Olivia's house, there was trouble brewing. Olivia's jester, Feste, had run away. Now he was back, and Olivia was very angry.

Malvolio, Olivia's steward, looked pleased that Feste was in trouble.

"You are supposed to be my jester." Olivia tapped her fingers on the arm of her chair. "Yet you have been missing for days! Why?"

Feste said nothing. Olivia's patience snapped. "Guards, take the fool away!"

The jester immediately pointed at Olivia. "You heard her, lads. Take her away."

Olivia stared at Feste. "I told them to take *you* away."

Feste put his hands on his hips. "No, my lady. You said, 'Take the fool away'. You are the biggest fool here, and I can prove it."

Olivia's lips twitched. "Do so, if you can."

Feste crossed his fingers. He was about to take a risk. "Why do you weep, my lady?"

Olivia gave him a hard stare. "For my dead brother, fool."

"I think his soul is in hell, my lady."

"I know his soul is in heaven!" snapped Olivia.

"Aha!" cried Feste. "Then you are a fool to weep for a soul in heaven."

Should I let this fool off, Malvolio?

You should have him hanged, my lady.

"Don't be so cruel, Malvolio," replied Olivia. "It is a fool's job to make us laugh at our own foolishness. You may go, Feste."

Feste hurried off. He was glad to have got off so lightly.

At that moment, Olivia's maid, Maria, hurried in. "Madam, there's a young man at the gate to see you."

Olivia shook her head. "I suppose he is bringing another message of love from Duke Orsino," she said. "Malvolio, go and let him in." She turned to Maria. "Let's have some fun with this messenger. Bring me two veils."

The messenger was Viola, in her page-boy disguise. When she was shown in, she saw two women. They were both wearing veils that hid their faces.

She paused. "Please – which of you is the Countess?"

Maria giggled. Olivia said, "Speak to me. What do you want?"

Most dear lady, whose beauty is greater than any words can say...

Maria snorted with laughter. Olivia pinched her. Viola stopped and looked at Olivia.

"Are you the Countess?" she asked. "I don't want to waste my speech. It took me ages to learn it."

"I am the Countess," said Olivia, "what do you wish to say?"

"My message is for your ears only," replied Viola.

Olivia nodded. She was becoming interested in this young man. She sent Maria away.

Viola stared at Olivia. So this was the woman Orsino loved. This was her rival!

"My lady," she said, "let me see your face."

"Very well." Olivia took off her veil.

Here is my face. You can tell your master you've seen it. Tell him it has the usual features – two red lips; two grey eyes with lids; one neck; one chin...

Viola's heart sank. She shook her head sadly. "I understand why my master loves you. You are beautiful."

Olivia suddenly felt shy and awkward. "I have told the Duke I cannot love him," she said.

"He will not accept that," said Viola angrily. "Nor would I. If I loved you as much as my master does, I would sing love songs outside your window all night. I would make you love me!"

Olivia gazed at the 'young man'. "Yes," she said. "I'm sure you would."

CHAPTER 5

Back from the dead

As Viola was leaving Olivia's house, two young men were talking in the town square nearby. One of them was Viola's twin brother, Sebastian. The other was the man who had rescued him from the sea. His name was Antonio. He was a sea captain and a deadly enemy of Duke Orsino.

"I must leave you now," said Sebastian.

"Why?" asked Antonio.

"I bring bad luck to everyone around me," Sebastian sighed. "When you rescued me from the sea, I was travelling with my twin sister, Viola. But our ship was wrecked and she was drowned."

Antonio bowed his head. "I'm sorry."

"Goodbye." Sebastian shook Antonio's hand and hurried away.

Duke Orsino's home town was a dangerous place for Antonio; but he couldn't leave his new friend alone in this strange country. He pulled up his hood and set off after Sebastian.

At the same moment, Viola came into the square behind him.

As she crossed the square, Viola felt a hand tap her shoulder. She swung round. It was Malvolio.

"My lady told me to give you this ring back," panted Malvolio. He was out of breath and angry at having to chase after Viola.

He held out a ring. Viola just stared at it.

She knew she hadn't given Olivia a ring.

Malvolio lost his temper. He threw the ring to the ground. "If you don't want it back, let it lie there until someone picks it up. Good day, sir."

Malvolio turned and stomped off.

Viola slowly reached down and picked up the ring. What did the countess mean by sending it to her?

Then she remembered her disguise.

Viola closed her eyes and let out a moan. Olivia thought that she was a man! "She's fallen in love with me!" groaned Viola. "What a mess!"

Orsino loved Olivia.

Viola loved Orsino. But because she was disguised as Cesario she could not tell him.

And now, Olivia loved 'Cesario'.

Viola shook her head sadly.

She was in a worse fix than ever, and she couldn't see any way out of it.

CHAPTER 6

The kill-joy

That night, at Olivia's house, Sir Toby Belch and Sir Andrew Aguecheek were getting drunk with Feste the jester.

They were singing at the top of their voices when Olivia's maid Maria burst in.

"What a racket!" Maria slapped Sir Toby with her apron. "Don't you know that the Countess has told Malvolio to throw you all out?"

Three Merry Men are we!

Sir Toby grabbed hold of Maria and began to dance with her.

But as they danced and sang...

Sir Toby glared at Malvolio. "Who do you think you are?" he thundered. "You misery-guts! Do you think that just because you're so dull, nobody else should have any fun?"

Malvolio shook with fury. He turned to Maria.

"Mistress Maria," he shouted. "You have been giving wine to these drunken fools. I am going to tell the Countess Olivia."

Malvolio slammed out of the room. Sir Toby gave a roar of rage, and ran after the steward. However, Maria stopped him.

"Let him go," she snapped. "If you cause any more trouble, my lady Olivia will throw you out. Leave Malvolio to me."

A wicked smile spread over Sir Toby's face. "What will you do?"

Maria's eyes glinted. "Malvolio is such a show-off, he already believes Olivia is in love with him. I'll write him a love letter. My handwriting is just like my lady Olivia's..."

Sir Toby clapped his hands. "So he'll think the letter is from my niece, and she fancies him!"

"Exactly! I'll make him look like a fool." Maria shook her finger at Sir Toby. "But no more noise tonight!"

CHAPTER 7

A love letter

The next day, Viola told Orsino the answer from Olivia.

"She still won't see me?" Orsino shook his head angrily. "Then you must go again, Cesario. Tell her my love is greater than the world..."

Viola held her hands out in appeal. "But what if she cannot love you, sir?"

The Duke clenched his fists. "I will not accept that answer!"

Viola felt an urge to hit him. "But you must! Suppose some other woman loved you as much as you love Olivia..."

The Duke shook his head. "No woman could love me as much as I love Olivia."

Viola was very angry. "Is that what you think? Then let me tell you..." She stopped suddenly.

Orsino stared at her. "Tell me what?" *31*

My father had a daughter. She loved a man. Just as much as I would love you ... if I was a woman.

Orsino sat beside her. "And what happened to her?"

"Nothing, my Lord. She never spoke of her love. She always smiled, but inside her heart was breaking." Viola turned away. "Shall I go to the lady?" she asked.

The Duke gave her a diamond. "Yes. Give her this. She will be mine, Cesario."

Viola took the jewel, and left without a word.

Meanwhile, back at Olivia's house, Maria had been busy. She found Sir Toby and Sir Andrew with a man called Fabian. Fabian also hated Malvolio. He had been Olivia's favourite servant until Malvolio had sacked him.

Maria pushed the three men behind a hedge. "You hide here," she said. "I'll drop the letter where Malvolio will find it." She put the letter in the middle of the path. Then she tiptoed away.

A few moments later, Malvolio came into view.

At that moment, Malvolio spotted Maria's letter.

He picked it up. "A letter addressed to 'M'." Malvolio looked around. "My lady has no other servants whose names begin with 'M'. It must be for me."

He tore the letter open, and began to read.

> *You are my servant, but I love you.*
>
> *Do not be afraid of greatness. Some are born great, some achieve greatness, and some have greatness thrust upon them.*
>
> *If you love me, wear yellow stockings tied with ribbons next time we meet.*
>
> *When you read this letter, you will know who I am.*
>
> *I love you. I love you.*
>
> *A friend.*

Malvolio gave a cry of joy, and ran off as fast as his legs could carry him.

Sir Toby, Sir Andrew and Fabian staggered from their hiding place. They laughed and laughed until their sides ached. When Maria arrived, Sir Toby flung his arms around her.

"Wonderful!" he cried. "Wait until Olivia sees Malvolio dressed up like a dog's dinner! She'll think he's gone mad."

Maria laughed. "She hates yellow stockings and ribbons! He'll look like a fool. Just you wait and see."

Fabian rubbed his hands together. "I wouldn't miss it for the world," he said grimly.

CHAPTER 8

Sir Andrew's challenge

Later that day, 'Cesario' brought another message from Orsino to Olivia.

Sir Toby and Sir Andrew saw 'Cesario' arriving. They decided to hide in the bushes again. They wanted to see what would happen.

"Give me your hand," Olivia said to 'Cesario'.

Viola held out her hand. Olivia took it.

"What is your name?"

"Cesario. The Duke has asked me to tell you that..."

"I do not want to hear what he has to say," snapped Olivia. "Do *you* have something to say to me?" she pleaded. Viola shook her head.

Olivia's voice became bitter. "Then I have no more time to waste. Go away."

Viola bowed to the Countess. "Goodbye. I will not visit you again."

Olivia ran after her. "But you must!

Perhaps you can change my mind about the Duke, after all..."

As soon as they had gone, Sir Andrew and Sir Toby stepped out from the bushes. They had heard every word.

"That's it!" cried Sir Andrew. "I shall go home tomorrow!"

Sir Toby pretended to be surprised, "Why?"

"Why? Why?" Sir Andrew waved his arms about. "Didn't you hear? Your niece loves the Duke's servant more than she loves me!"

Sir Toby sighed. "Dear Sir Andrew. You don't understand women, do you? My niece is just pretending to be in love with that boy."

Sir Andrew looked puzzled. "Why?"

Sir Toby smiled sweetly. "She wants you to show how brave you are. She wants you to challenge him to a duel!"

Sir Andrew thought about this. "Are you sure?"

"Of course," lied Sir Toby.

Just then Maria ran in. "Malvolio's dressed in yellow stockings and ribbons! He's on his way to see Olivia. Let's hide in the bushes and watch what happens."

Sir Toby grinned like a wolf. "That's what bushes are for!"

CHAPTER 9

Malvolio goes mad

Olivia watched Cesario disappear down the road. She closed the gate, turned ... and felt her jaw drop. "Malvolio?" she said.

Olivia backed away. Malvolio must have been working too hard. He had clearly lost his mind. She gave him a nervous smile.

"Would you like to go to bed, Malvolio?" she said kindly.

Malvolio's eyes bulged. "To bed! Oh, yes, sweetheart, I'll go to bed with you!"

What?!

Some are born great!

Maria rushed out from her hiding place. "Malvolio," she cried, "what are you doing?"

Olivia pulled herself free from Malvolio. "Maria, call Sir Toby. Tell him to look after Malvolio." She hurried away.

Sir Toby and Fabian stepped forward.

Malvolio looked down his nose at them. "Go and hang yourselves!" he snapped. "I am a greater man than any of you."

He strode away with his nose in the air.

"Ha!" said Sir Toby. "I'll look after the poor madman, all right. I'll lock him in the darkest, dirtiest room in the palace. Let's see how the 'great man' likes that!" He rubbed his hands. "Then we'll see about Sir Andrew's duel with Cesario!"

Maria shook her finger at him. "If Sir Andrew hurts Cesario, Olivia will be very angry."

"Don't worry," said Fabian. "Sir Andrew couldn't hurt a fly." He grinned. "But Cesario doesn't know that!"

CHAPTER 10

The duel

Elsewhere in town, Viola's brother Sebastian frowned at his friend Antonio. "What am I to do with you?" he said. "I told you not to follow me."

Antonio grinned. "I couldn't leave you to get into trouble."

Sebastian laughed. "I'm glad to see you. Well, what shall we do? Go and see the sights?"

Antonio looked around carefully. "You go. It would be dangerous for me to be seen here. I sank some of Orsino's ships, recently. I don't think he'd be pleased to see me."

"Then you'd better stay out of sight."

Antonio nodded. "I will. I'll go and book some rooms at the inn. You can join me later." He gave his purse to Sebastian. "You might want to buy something. You can pay me back when we meet again. Goodbye."

A few streets away, Viola was on her way back to Duke Orsino when Sir Toby and Fabian caught up with her.

"Prepare to defend yourself, sir," said Sir Toby. "You have offended the most dangerous swordsman in Illyria. He is waiting for you by the orchard."

Viola was horrified. "But I haven't offended anybody."

"But you have," replied Sir Toby. "Fabian, stay here with this gentleman. I will fetch Sir Andrew."

Viola began to shake with fear. Sir Toby marched away to speak to Sir Andrew.

"I think you're in trouble," he said, shaking his head. "This fellow Cesario is an expert swordsman."

Then I'm not going to fight him!

It's too late. You can't back out now.

Sir Toby and Fabian pushed Sir Andrew and Viola towards each other. Then they stood back to watch the fun.

Just then, Antonio came round the corner, and stopped dead. It looked as though his friend Sebastian was in trouble!

Antonio charged down the street. His sword flashed in the sunlight.

Sir Toby drew his sword ready to fight Antonio.

"Sir Toby," cried Fabian, "put away your sword! Here come the Duke's guards."

Sir Toby glared at Antonio. "I've not finished with you yet."

The Duke's guards surrounded Antonio.

"Antonio, I arrest you in the Duke's name."

With a sigh, Antonio dropped his sword. He turned to Viola.

"I'm sorry. I must have my purse back."

Viola gazed at him in astonishment. "But I don't have your purse."

Antonio gritted his teeth. "I rescued you from death. Is this how you pay me back? I will have my revenge!"

With a final glare at Viola, Antonio was led away.

Viola was confused. The stranger had obviously mistaken her for someone else. But who?

It couldn't be her brother Sebastian. He was dead.

Sir Toby watched as Viola wandered away in a daze. "That boy's a coward," he said.

Sir Andrew's face lit up. "Then I'll chase after him, and beat him black and blue." He picked up his sword and chased after 'Cesario'.

Sir Toby and Fabian followed, grinning like crocodiles.

CHAPTER 11

Mistaken identity

Sir Andrew found 'Cesario' outside Olivia's house. He pulled a glove from his belt, and slapped the young man across the face.

Unfortunately for Sir Andrew, he hadn't found Viola. He had found Sebastian! Sebastian slapped him back.

Suddenly, Sebastian felt a hand on his shoulder. "Calm down, sir," growled Sir Toby.

"Let me go!" Sebastian drew his sword.

The noise brought Olivia to her door. She looked out. Her uncle was fighting again! And the person he was fighting looked like Cesario!

"Toby! Put down your sword and get out of my sight!" she ordered. Olivia turned to Sebastian. "You're not hurt are you, dear Cesario?"

Sebastian stared at Olivia. He didn't know why she called him 'Cesario'. But it didn't matter. She was the most beautiful woman he had ever seen.

Olivia gazed at him. "Have you changed your mind? Do you think you could love me?"

Sebastian stared into Olivia's eyes. "Love you? Oh, yes. I think I could."

With a cry of joy, Olivia flung her arms around him.

CHAPTER 12

Twelfth night

Later that afternoon, Antonio stood facing Duke Orsino.

Orsino's gaze was as hard as stone. "Why are you here, Antonio?"

"I came to your country to protect that boy." Antonio pointed at Viola. "Some weeks ago, I rescued him from the sea. Since then, we have been friends. I lent him my purse and defended him in a fight. Now he says he doesn't know me."

The Duke's lip curled. "You're mad. This youth is my servant."

At that moment Olivia swept into the court. Orsino stood and bowed.

Olivia's voice was cold. "I did not come here to see you, my lord," she said. "I came to see Cesario."

Viola stared at her.

Olivia turned to Viola. "Why have you gone back to Orsino, Cesario? This morning, you promised you would never leave me."

Orsino looked from Olivia to Viola. "What does this mean, Cesario?" said the Duke, "Have you stolen my love from me?" His fingers gripped his dagger. "Come with me!" he ordered.

Viola turned to follow him.

Olivia ran forward. "Cesario, don't go!"

Viola's eyes were filled with pain. "I must."

"Why?"

"Because I love him!"

Olivia began to cry. "Cesario, you are my husband. Stay with me!"

Orsino stared at Olivia. "Her husband?" he whispered.

"Yes, my husband!"

The Duke turned to Viola. He was trembling with rage. "Is this true?"

Viola was stunned. "No, my lord!"

"We were married two hours ago." Olivia held out her hand to Viola. "Don't be afraid, Cesario. Come with me."

Before the Duke could say anything else, Sir Toby and Sir Andrew limped in.

Viola stared at them in amazement. "You're lying. You tried to pick a fight with me, but I didn't hurt you."

"You did!" Sir Andrew said. "Didn't he, Sir Toby?" He tried to hide behind the fat Knight.

Sir Toby lost his temper. "You ass! You fool!" Roaring with rage, he chased Sir Andrew out of the hall.

At that moment, Sebastian came in.

He bowed to Olivia. "Madam, I'm sorry I have hurt your uncle. I had to defend myself..." He noticed Antonio, who was staring at him as if he'd seen a ghost. "Antonio! I've been trying to find you. I've still got your purse..."

Sebastian stopped. He realised that everyone was staring at him and at the young man standing beside the Duke...

Sebastian finally saw Viola.

He dropped his sword.

59

Viola took her brother's hands. "I am your sister Viola."

With a cry of joy, Sebastian threw his arms around Viola.

People all started talking at once. They could hardly believe what they were seeing.

But there was one more surprise.

A dirty figure walked into the court. It was Malvolio. He stood before Olivia. His voice was bitter. "Madam, you have done me wrong."

He gave Olivia the letter Maria had written. "You sent me this letter. You made me think that you were in love with me. I did what you told me to do. But you treated me as a madman. You had me locked in a dark room. Why?"

Olivia looked at him with pity. "This is not my writing. Maria wrote this letter."

Fabian stepped forward. "My lady, Sir Toby and I played this trick on Malvolio. We felt he needed to be brought down a peg or two."

Malvolio turned and walked slowly from the court. Olivia shook her head sadly.

Then she turned to Sebastian. "It seems that I married you by mistake." She gave Viola a sad smile. "But that mistake has saved me from a worse one."

Orsino took Viola's hand. "Cesario was my servant, and my friend. But you are no longer Cesario. Now you are Viola. Will you be my wife?"

And so, all the tricks and disguises came to an end. Olivia was married to Sebastian. Orsino married Viola. Sir Toby married Maria.

But did they live happily ever after? Or did Malvolio return to have his revenge? Sadly, this story does not say.

For all tales must have an ending.

And this is...

The End

William Shakespeare was an actor as well as a playwright. He must have enjoyed the make-believe of the stage.

When he wrote his plays, four hundred years ago, the Christmas holidays went on for twelve days. People would dress up and play games. Everybody would pretend to be someone else.

On the twelfth night after Christmas, these games would end. People had to go back to being themselves. That is why Shakespeare called this play *Twelfth Night*.

Steve Barlow and **Steve Skidmore** wrote this story from Shakespeare's play. They like reading Shakespeare. "Why not?" they say. "He's the greatest writer ever."

They have also adapted *Romeo and Juliet* for **High Impact**.